Tortoise Soup!

Retold by Dawn McMillan

Illustrations by Chantal Stewart

Contents

Rigby®

HOUGHTON MIFFLIN HARCOURT
Supplemental Publishers

www.Rigby.com
800-531-5015

Chapter 1

Where Is Goat?

Once there were four very good friends,
Tortoise, Goat, Raven, and Rat.
They lived in a forest.

Every morning, Tortoise crawled out of his burrow
and slowly made his way down to the river
for a drink of water.
There he met Goat, Raven, and Rat,
who liked to drink from the river, too.

Goat, Raven, and Rat could move much faster than Tortoise and they got to the river first. But they always waited patiently for their friend to arrive.

Every day, Raven croaked, "Here he comes!"
and then Tortoise and his friends
would drink together.

One morning, when Tortoise reached the river, he saw Raven and Rat sitting on the riverbank looking very sad.

"What's wrong?" asked Tortoise anxiously.

"Goat is late," answered Rat.

"Goat is never late!" exclaimed Tortoise.

"Maybe Goat is sick," suggested Raven.

"We must do something," said Rat.
"I'll search for her along the riverbank."

Raven spread her wings and called,
"I'll fly around to see if I can find her!"

"I'll wait here in case she is late," said Tortoise quietly.

Chapter 2

To the Rescue

When Raven returned, she called to Rat,
"You won't find Goat by the river.
Goat has been caught in a hunter's net nearby!"

"Oh, no!" cried Tortoise in despair.

"We must help her to escape!" said Rat quickly.
"Raven, take me to her
so I can bite through the net."

"Good idea, Rat," replied Raven.
"Climb up on my back and we'll go find Goat!
Wait here, Tortoise. Try not to worry.
We'll do our best to save her!"

"Here we are, Goat!" Raven called
as she and Rat landed beside Goat.
"We've come to save you!
Stay still and Rat will bite through the net.
Soon you'll be free."

"Oh, thank you," said Goat.
"I'm so glad to see you both.
Please hurry, Rat. The hunter will be here soon!"

Rat chewed and chewed.
When he was through the last of the ropes,
he looked up to see Tortoise plodding toward them.

"Tortoise!" exclaimed Rat.
"What are you doing here?
This is not a safe place for you!
Raven told you to wait at the riverbank."

"I had to come," Tortoise said, puffing.
"You are my friends, and I was worried about you!"

Chapter 3

Goat Gets Away

At that very moment, the hunter arrived.

"Run, Goat!" Rat called loudly.
Goat scrambled to her feet and raced away.

"My net is ruined!" exclaimed the hunter
as he stared at the chewed net. "And the goat is gone!"

Rat scrambled into a hole and Raven flew high into
the sky, but Tortoise was too slow to escape.

"Oh, well," the hunter said with a moan.
"I don't have a goat to eat, but I do have a tortoise.
Tortoise soup is very tasty!"

With that, the hunter scooped up Tortoise
and put him in his bag.

As the hunter walked away,
Goat ran back to Rat and Raven.

"Poor Tortoise!" exclaimed Rat.

"Tortoise soup!" Raven said anxiously.

"It's no use sitting here crying!" whispered Goat. "Our tears will do Tortoise no good at all. We must help him to escape. I have a plan. Listen carefully!"

Chapter 4

Saving Tortoise

Goat raced toward the hunter.
She hid behind a tree, and then she hobbled out
in front of him.

"There's that goat!" exclaimed the hunter.
"She's hurt, so I should be able to catch her!"

The hunter dropped his bag and chased after Goat.
Sometimes Goat allowed him to come very close,
but then she hobbled out of reach again.

As Goat led the hunter away,
Rat and Raven hurried to help Tortoise.

"Quick!" Raven called out to Rat.
"Tug at that rope and undo the bag!"

"There!" said Rat as the bag came undone.
"Come on, Tortoise!
Hide in the bushes with me!"

When Tortoise was free, Raven flew to Goat and screamed, "Run!"

The hunter couldn't believe his eyes.
"That goat wasn't hurt at all!" he said angrily
as he watched Goat disappear into the forest.
"I guess I will just have to make do with
tortoise soup."

But when the hunter returned to his bag,
it was empty.

"Ha!" Raven said, laughing as she flew
above the hunter's head.
"No goat for your dinner, and no tortoise soup, either!"

The next morning, when the four friends met, they were very happy to see one another.

"Thank you for saving me yesterday," said Goat.

"Me, too," said Tortoise.
"I didn't like the idea of tortoise soup!"

"Good friends always help one another," replied Raven.

"Yes," said Rat. "That's what friends are for!"